This Storybook Belongs To

Princess _____

Beauty and the Beast

Once upon a time on a cold, stormy night, an old woman begged at a Prince's door. She offered the Prince a rose, but he selfishly told her to go away. Suddenly—the beggar magically changed into a beautiful enchantress, much to the Prince's surprise. Then, because of his selfishness, she cast a spell on him, turning the Prince into a hideous beast.

The spell would be broken, and the prince would become human again, only if he could learn to love another and earn that person's love in return. But who could ever learn to love a beast?

In a small village, not too far from the Beast's castle, lived a young woman named Belle. Belle loved books more than anything. While everyone in town admired the handsome hunter, Gaston, Belle kept her nose buried in her favorite books.

This bothered Gaston, for he intended to marry Belle. "After all," he explained, "she's the best. And, don't I deserve the best?"

Belle knew that she could never care for anyone as conceited and as selfish as Gaston.

The villagers all thought that Belle was strange. And they thought that her father, Maurice the inventor, was even stranger.

Maurice was hard at work on his newest invention: a machine that chopped wood by itself.

"You are sure to win first prize at the fair tomorrow, Papa!" said Belle, seeing him off. "Good-bye! Good luck!"

Poor Maurice never arrived at the fair, for he got lost along the way. Separated from his horse, Phillipe, Maurice made his way to the Beast's enchanted castle.

In the castle, a talking clock named Cogsworth and candelabrum named Lumiere greeted Maurice. The same spell that had turned the Prince into a beast had also turned his servants into objects.

The Beast soon discovered Maurice and took him prisoner.

When Phillipe returned home alone, Belle knew that her father was in trouble. She asked the horse to lead her to Maurice. He led Belle back to the Beast's dark castle.

"What is this place?" asked Belle, walking down the hallway. "Papa!" she called out.

Maurice called out to Belle, and she found him locked away. Then Belle also met the angry Beast.

The Beast roared when the frightened young woman asked him to free her father. "He's my prisoner!" yelled the Beast.

Mustering up all her courage, Belle whispered, "If I take his place, will you let him go?"

The Beast agreed. "But you must promise to stay here forever," he told her.
Terrified of the Beast, Belle replied, "You have my word."

Now that Belle would be staying in the castle, she decided to have a look around. Even though the Beast had warned her to stay away, she wandered into the forbidden West Wing. There, she found the enchanted rose that held the Beast's fate: he had to learn to love another and earn that person's love in return before the last petal fell. If he did not, he would remain a Beast forever.

Suddenly, the Beast appeared behind her and screamed, "Get out!" He was afraid that Belle would touch the rose and cause the petal to fall before its time.

Belle was so frightened that she took Phillipe and ran from the castle, trying to get away as quickly as she could. But they were soon surrounded by hungry, terrifying wolves.

Grabbing a stick, Belle tried to defend herself, but the wolves were too strong. Before she could scream, the Beast appeared and fought off the wolves himself. He was hurt, but he had saved Belle's life.

Back inside the castle, Belle tended to the Beast's wounds, realizing that he wasn't really so scary. He just had a very bad temper.

In time, Belle and the Beast became friends. They read together in the library, fed the birds together outside, and even danced together.

One day, the Beast asked if Belle was happy. She told him that she would be, if only she could see her father. The Beast showed her a magic mirror, and Maurice appeared, looking ill.

"Papa is sick!" cried Belle. "I must go to him."

The Beast loved Belle and thought only about her happiness. He released her, giving her the mirror to take home, so she could look in it and see him anytime she liked.

Meanwhile, back in the village, Maurice had been trying to rally the villagers to rescue Belle from the Beast. Everyone thought Maurice was crazy, and they didn't believe him. But Gaston found a way to use Belle's father to his advantage. He would have him declared crazy and locked up forever…or at least until Belle agreed to marry him.

Belle hurried home to her father and, to prove he wasn't crazy, she showed Gaston and the villagers the Beast's image in the magic mirror. Gaston convinced everyone to follow him and destroy the hideous monster that lived close by.

When Gaston and the villagers arrived at the castle, they were met with a surprise. All the enchanted objects in the castle came together to defend their master and their home.

Gaston decided to take on the Beast himself. He and the Beast fought.
Gaston lost his footing and fell from the castle roof, but not before badly
injuring the Beast.

By the time Belle could get to him, the Beast lay dying. Deep within the West Wing of the castle, the enchanted rose was about to lose its last remaining petal.

"Please don't leave me," Belle said, sobbing over the Beast's body. "I love you." Through her tears, Belle saw the Beast magically transform.

The spell was broken! The enchanted objects returned to their human form.
The Beast once again became the Prince he used to be, but love had restored
kindness to his heart. He was now handsome inside and out.

Belle and her prince danced together, knowing that they would both live
happily ever after.